Unicorn Magic

Glitterhoof's Secret Garden

Daisy Meadows

ORCHARD

Special thanks to Elizabeth Galloway

ORCHARD BOOKS

First published in Great Britain in 2019 by The Watts Publishing Group

1 3 5 7 9 10 8 6 4 2

Text copyright © 2019 Working Partners Limited.
Illustrations © Orchard Books 2019
Series created by Working Partners Limited

A CIP catalogue record for this book is available from the British Library.

ISBN 978 1 40835 696 8

Printed and bound in Australia by McPhersons Printing Group

The paper and board used in this book are made from wood from responsible sources.

Orchard Books
An imprint of Hachette Children's Group
Part of The Watts Publishing Group Limited
Carmelite House
50 Victoria Embankment
London EC4Y 0DZ

An Hachette UK Company
www.hachette.co.uk
www.hachettechildrens.co.uk

Contents

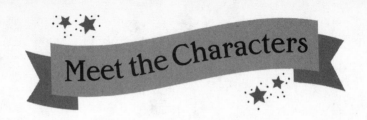

Aisha and Emily are best friends from Spellford Village. Aisha loves sports, whilst Emily's favourite thing is science. But what both girls enjoy more than anything is visiting Enchanted Valley and helping their unicorn friends who live there.

Dawnblaze is the Fire Unicorn. She loves to swim in the hot springs on Firework Mountain with her dragon friends!

Dawnblaze

The Air Unicorn, Shimmerbreeze, is in charge of making sure the air in Enchanted Valley is fresh and clean. She likes to use her magic to create little breezes, so her friends can fly their kites.

Shimmerbreeze

Glitterhoof is the Earth Unicorn, who makes plants grow strong and beautiful. What she likes best is being part of a team – there's nothing she won't do for her friends!

Glitterhoof

Sparklesplash has so much fun playing in the rivers and lagoons of Enchanted Valley. This Water Unicorn wants everyone to love the water, just as much as she does.

Sparklesplash

An Enchanted Valley lies a twinkle away,
Where beautiful unicorns live, laugh and play
You can visit the mermaids, or go for a ride,
So much fun to be had, but dangers can hide!

Your friends need your help ~ this is how you know:
A keyring lights up with a magical glow.
Whirled off like a dream, you won't want to leave.
Friendship forever, when you truly believe.

Chapter One
Rainy Day Magic

Rain pattered hard against the windows of Enchanted Cottage.

"I don't think we'll be playing football today," said Aisha Khan with a sigh. She and her best friend, Emily Turner, were watching the rain from the warm kitchen. Drops fell from the flowers in the

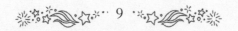

garden, and trickled over the wings of the phoenix statue in the middle of the lawn.

"Don't worry," Emily said with a grin. "I know what we can do instead!"

Aisha smiled back. "A science experiment?"

"How did you guess?" Emily laughed. She loved science as much as Aisha loved sport. "First we need some flowers …"

The two girls darted out of the back door into the wet garden. They hadn't known each other long, as Aisha and her

parents had only recently moved into Enchanted Cottage. But already they did everything together – and they had even shared some magical adventures …

The girls picked a handful of flowers. Then they ran back indoors, shaking rain from their hair.

Soon Aisha's mum had helped the girls set up their experiment. On the kitchen table were several small bowls of water, with a few drops of food colouring in each one. The girls put the flowers in the coloured water.

"What happens now?" asked Aisha.

"Wait and see," said Emily with a smile. The two girls drank hot chocolate and chatted with Mrs Khan, who was stirring a saucepan of curry on the stove. After a while, Mrs Khan pointed at the flowers. "Girls, look!"

Aisha gasped. The flowers were changing colour! The yellow petals were turning blue and the pink petals were turning green.

"They're drinking up the food colouring," Emily explained with a grin.

Aisha peered closely at some white petals, now edged with pink. "It's almost like magic," she whispered.

Emily knew they were both thinking about the same thing – Enchanted Valley, the magical realm they had visited, which was filled with unicorns and other amazing creatures!

A glint of light
caught Emily's eye,
and she gasped –
the unicorn keyring
hanging from
Aisha's belt loop
was glowing! Aisha
noticed the light as
well, and clasped her hand around the
little unicorn. Emily pulled her matching
keyring from the front pocket of her
dungarees. It was glowing too.

Queen Aurora, a beautiful unicorn who
ruled over Enchanted Valley, was calling
them back!

"Er, Mum," said Aisha, "we're just going
to get some more flowers …"

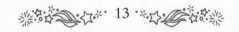

Mrs Khan was busy tasting the curry with a spoon. "Don't get too wet!" she said.

Aisha and Emily hurried back outside. Even though it was still raining, a shaft of sunlight shone through a break in the clouds, beaming on to the lawn beside the phoenix statue. The girls ran over to it. They touched the horns of their unicorn keyrings together and – *whooosh!* – rainbow-coloured sparkles shimmered around them.

"We're going to see the unicorns!" cried Emily. Excitement fizzed through them like fireworks. They held hands as the sparkles swirled faster and faster, and their feet left the ground. Clouds of the

whizzing sparkles surrounded them, red,
blue, purple and yellow, and the girls
could feel their hair being blown around
them as they were carried far away …

When the sparkles faded, the girls sank
gently back to the ground. They stood in
a beautiful meadow of soft grass under a
clear blue sky. Ahead of them was a green
hill topped with a golden palace. Flags

fluttered from its four turrets.

"It's so great to be here again," said Aisha. "But we'd better hurry – Queen Aurora might need our help!"

"I hope Selena hasn't come back," said Emily, with a frown.

The thought of the wicked unicorn made the girls shiver as they made their way up the hill towards the palace. They had already helped Queen Aurora by finding two of the unicorns' magical lockets, which Selena had stolen because she wanted to rule Enchanted Valley. But Selena still had two more lockets, and she was sure to cause trouble with them ...

Even so, the girls couldn't help feeling a rush of happiness as they climbed higher

and saw Enchanted Valley spread out all around. There were soft green fields, glittering lakes and majestic forests, while mysterious purple mountains stood on the horizon.

Emily pointed up at a bird-like creature fluttering over the forest, just like the statue in the cottage garden. It was followed by several little chicks. "That must be Ember and her family!" she said with a grin. The girls had helped the phoenix on their last visit to Enchanted Valley. "I wonder what creatures we'll meet this time?"

At the top of the hill the palace stood before them, its golden walls gleaming. Silver flowers grew over it, and the

windows glittered like diamonds. A moat
of crystal-clear water ran around the
palace, with a drawbridge lying across
it. But the most magical sight of all was

the beautiful unicorn standing on the drawbridge. Her body shimmered with all the colours of the dawn – she was a dusky pink one moment, vivid orange the next, and then as golden as the palace itself. Her horn gleamed, and a silver crown sat on top of her head.

"Queen Aurora!" cried the girls.

"Welcome back, Emily and Aisha!" replied the unicorn, her voice lilting like beautiful music. "Thank goodness you're here … because we need your help again!"

Chapter Two
Sneezes and Stormclouds

Queen Aurora led the girls over the drawbridge and through a grassy courtyard. They followed her under an arch of roses and into a pretty garden. Cherry trees were dotted around, their blossoms falling like confetti, and there were rose bushes with sweet-scented blooms. Gathered at a table in the centre of the garden were four unicorns the girls recognised – the Nature Unicorns! They looked up as the girls and Aurora approached.

"Hello, girls!" said a unicorn, with a bright orange mane.

"It's so nice to see you!" said the white unicorn.

"Hi, Dawnblaze! Hi, Shimmerbreeze!" said Emily and Aisha.

"It's wonderful to see you too," added Aisha, as both girls hugged them.

Around every unicorn's neck hung a glass locket which gave them the magic they needed to protect a part of Enchanted Valley. Dawnblaze's locket

contained tiny fireworks — she was the
fire unicorn, and kept the valley warm.
Shimmerbreeze the air unicorn kept the
air clean, and her locket contained tiny
fluffy clouds. Queen Aurora protected
friendship — inside her locket were two
tiny suns that spun around each other,
just like friends playing.

Emily and Aisha had got Dawnblaze's

and Shimmerbreeze's lockets back from horrible Selena after she'd stolen them. But the other two unicorns were still missing theirs. The girls hugged them too. "Hi, Glitterhoof!" they said. "Hi, Sparklesplash!"

Dipping her horn, Glitterhoof the Earth Unicorn picked up two flower garlands from the pile heaped on the table. She was leaf-green with a lilac mane and tail. "We're making these to give to the guests at the Nature Gala," she explained. The Nature Gala was a party the unicorns were throwing for all their Enchanted Valley friends.

Sparklesplash, the blue Water Unicorn who protected the lakes and rivers, flicked

her silver tail. "Try them on, girls!"

They lowered their heads and
Glitterhoof placed the flower garlands
over them. Emily's was made of yellow
roses, while Aisha's had white daisies.
But as soon as the garlands were hung
around the girls' necks, their petals began
to droop. The girls watched in dismay
as, one by one, the flowers fell from the

garlands on to the ground.

"Oh, not again!" said Glitterhoof. Her ears drooped too.

Queen Aurora sighed. "This is why I asked you to come today, girls," she said. "Glitterhoof's locket usually makes the soil rich and the plants beautiful, but without it, the plants are suffering. I'm worried that if we don't get it back soon, all the plants in Enchanted Valley will die."

Emily and Aisha both shook their heads in dismay. Looking around the garden, they realised that Aurora was right – the plants here were already wilting. The blossoms falling from the cherry trees were brown and the roses were limp.

"We can't let that happen," said
Aisha fiercely. "We'll find your locket,
Glitterhoof."

But just then, grey clouds rolled over the
sky and turned it as dark as night. The air
was suddenly chilly. Lightning crackled,
making them all jump, and a burst of
thunder like beating drums rumbled
overhead.

In the darkness appeared a silver
unicorn. She shone like the moon, and
her mane and tail were deep blue. She
landed in the garden, her purple eyes
flashing as she looked around at the
horrified girls and the unicorns. It was
Selena!

"Oh n-n-n-no!" stammered Glitterhoof.

Her four legs quivered with fright.

Aisha and Emily were trembling too, but they huddled close to Glitterhoof. "We won't let Selena do anything mean to you," said Emily, putting her arms around the green unicorn's neck.

"It's n-n-n-not that," said Glitterhoof. "It's the d-d-d-dark that's so scary!"

"Quiet!" snapped Selena. She reared up on her hind legs

and the tiny storm inside her glass locket flashed. "So you girls are back, are you? Well, no matter. You can't stop me this time!"

"Yes, we can!" cried Aisha bravely.

Selena gave a cackle that echoed like the thunder. "You'll never get the Earth locket back!" She looked around, scowling. "Flit? Flit, get over here!"

"Aaaaah-choooo!" An enormous sneeze came from the other side of the palace wall. Then a little black bat shot over. It was Flit, Selena's naughty helper. He landed among the flower garlands and wiped his nose with his wing.

The girls gasped. Around Flit's neck hung Glitterhoof's locket, with its purple

flower growing inside!

"Aaaaah-choooo!" Flit's sneeze sent
him flying off the table. He landed in one
of the cherry trees. "Aaaaah-choooo!"
He fell on to the lawn and wiped his nose
again.

"Oh, stop that silly sneezing, Flit," said
Selena crossly, stamping a hoof.

"Sobby, Sebena," said Flit, sniffing
loudly. "All bees flowers are bunging

up by nose. I can't wait for bem to disappear."

"And you're going to make sure they do," said Selena. She sneered at the other unicorns. "Flit's going to hide the locket where you will never find it! The plants will die – and I will only bring them back if you make me the Queen of Enchanted Valley! Ha!"

She reared up again and slammed her hooves on the lawn. The girls and the unicorns cried out in alarm as the ground began to shake. The flower garlands fell off the table. Aisha and Emily had to hold tight to Glitterhoof to keep from falling.

Queen Aurora reared up too, her silver horn flashing. "You will never rule

Enchanted Valley, Selena!"

"We'll see about that!" cackled Selena. She took off, spiralling up into the air until she disappeared among the thunderclouds.

Emily leaped back as her foot slipped suddenly. "Look out!" she yelled. The ground where Selena had slammed her hooves was crumbling away to make a deep sinkhole. The hole quickly spread. The table and flower garlands fell into it, and then one of the cherry trees.

"Girls, climb on to Glitterhoof," cried Queen Aurora. "Hurry!"

The girls scrambled on to Glitterhoof's back, Aisha pulling up Emily behind her. All the unicorns took off just as the ground under their feet fell away completely. Nothing was left of the centre of the garden but an enormous hole.

Glitterhoof shook her head sadly. "It's all because I haven't got my locket," she said. "Instead of the earth being protected, it's being destroyed!"

"This is terrible," said Emily. "We must

stop Selena before things get worse."

Above them flapped Flit, his sneezes sending him zigzagging across the sky. Now that Selena had gone, the storm clouds drifted away. Glitterhoof gave a whinny of relief as the sunshine returned, allowing them a clear view as Flit disappeared over the palace wall, the stolen locket around his neck.

Aisha pointed after him. "Come on, Glitterhoof – let's follow that bat!"

Chapter Three
Caught!

"Good luck, girls!" called Queen Aurora. She was flying too, circling the ruined palace garden with the other unicorns. "Good luck, Glitterhoof!"

"Thank you!" the girls and Glitterhoof called back. Then they turned and soared after Flit. Aisha held tight to the unicorn's

mane, while Emily held on to Aisha's
waist. Glitterhoof's lilac tail fluttered in
the wind like streamers. From up high,
they could see more sinkholes appearing
among the forests and meadows, like an
outbreak of chickenpox spots.

Ahead, Flit began sneezing again.
"Aaaaah-choooo! Aaaaah-choooo!
Aaaaah-CHOOO!" The final sneeze sent
him plummeting down towards a patch
of trees. As he fell, the stolen locket glinted

in the sun.

"Hold on tight!" called Glitterhoof, and
she dropped after him in a steep dive.
The air whistled past Emily and Aisha's
ears as they flew down, down, down and
hurtled after Flit into the trees. Ahead, the
little bat had recovered himself, and was
flapping through the tree trunks.

Glitterhoof's hooves struck the ground
with a jolt, and the girls clung on tight.
The unicorn cantered after Flit. All

around, the leaves from the trees were falling, and many branches were already bare.

"Sinkhole!" shouted Aisha.

It opened in front of them like a hungry mouth. Glitterhoof jumped into the air to clear it – but was suddenly yanked back down to the forest floor. Aisha and Emily screamed, and Glitterhoof whinnied, as they were thrown sprawling to the grond.

"What happened?" gasped Emily, sitting up and shaking leaves from her hair.

"Oh no, Glitterhoof!" Aisha scrambled over to the unicorn. She was sitting on her haunches, with a vine looped tightly around her front leg. "Are you all right?"

"I'm not hurt," Glitterhoof said. "But I

can't get this horrible thing off! It grew
out of the hole and grabbed me." The
vine began to writhe around like a snake,
dragging Glitterhoof towards the sinkhole.

Above them, Flit flew a loop-the-loop.
"Sibby unicorn!" he giggled. "Sibby girls!
Now you'll neber catch me! Aaaaah-
choooo!" He disappeared among the
trees, taking the locket with him.

Aisha yanked hard at the vine,
untangling the knot it had made around

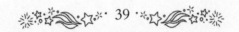

Glitterhoof's leg. The girls grinned with relief as the vine slithered back into the sinkhole and Glitterhoof got to her hooves.

"Thank you!" the unicorn said. Then her ears twitched with worry. "But I'm afraid Flit was right – we've lost him."

They carried on through the forest, past more sinkholes and forest flowers that had lost their petals. But with no sign of Flit, they weren't sure what to do next. Soon, Glitterhoof's violet eyes filled with tears.

"There must be someone who can help us," said Emily.

Aisha suddenly sprinted ahead. "There is!" she cried. "Come on!"

Emily and Glitterhoof hurried after her.

Walking down a path at the edge of the forest was a familiar little creature. He wore a long purple gown and a pointed hat with silver stars, and he was pulling a wooden cart along with a rope.

"Hob!" cried Emily. The girls had met Hob the goblin on their previous visits to Enchanted Valley. He had made them magical potions, which had helped them get back the lockets of Dawnblaze and Shimmerbreeze.

Hob took off his gold spectacles and polished them with the sleeve of his gown. When

he put them back on, his wrinkly green face beamed at them. "Bless my stars!" he said. "If it isn't Aisha and Emily, and Glitterhoof too! What brings you here?"

Glitterhoof dipped her horn in greeting, while the girls stooped to give Hob a hug. He was only half as tall as they were.

Aisha quickly explained about Flit and the stolen locket. "But what are you doing here, Hob?" asked Aisha. The girls knew that their friend rarely left the cave where he created his magical potions.

Hob pointed to his cart, which was stacked high with empty jars and bottles. "None of my potion ingredients are working properly," he explained, "so I'm collecting some new ones." He took off

his hat and scratched his bald green head.
"Oh, it has been very tiresome! I heated
up a cauldron of snugberries to make a
magic hot water bottle, and do you know
what happened?"

"What?" asked the girls and Glitterhoof.

"I popped the hot water bottle into my
bed, but when I got under the blankets
with my copy of *Peppers and Pickles for
Perfect Potions*, it wasn't lovely and snug
at all." He shuddered. "The snugberries
had all gone hard and lumpy! And they
weren't warm at all. It quite ruined my
nap."

Aisha hid a smile. "That sounds
horrible, Hob."

"It must have been because of my

missing locket," said Glitterhoof.

Hob nodded. "I bet that's it. I'm on my way to Flowerdew Garden to fetch some more ingredients," he said. "That's where all the magical plants in the valley come from. I just hope it's still all right."

"We'll come too," said Aisha. "Maybe we can find a magical plant that will help us get the locket back."

They all set off down the path, taking it in turns to pull Hob's cart. The jars and bottles jangled as they crossed a meadow

full of wilting grass, then a shallow stream. "We're almost there," said Hob. "But oh, piddleprickles – look at that!"

Ahead was a walled garden with a wooden door and plants growing all around it. But between the garden and the four friends were sinkholes – lots of them! There were so many holes that there was barely any grass left. From each hole writhed the same horrible vines that had almost caught Glitterhoof.

"Why are there so many sinkholes

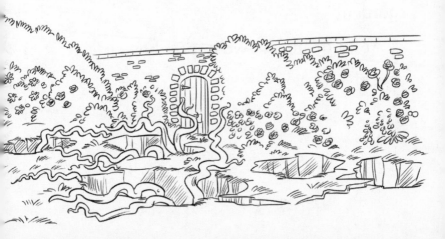

here?" asked Glitterhoof.

Emily and Aisha glanced at each other, eyes widening. "I think I know," said Emily. "Selena's horrible magic makes the lockets have the opposite effect they're supposed to. The closer you get to the locket, the worse the magic gets."

Aisha nodded. "These are definitely the worst sinkholes we've seen …"

"… which must mean Glitterhoof's locket is close by," Emily said, with a rush of excitement. "I bet it's inside the garden!"

Aisha grinned. "We'll soon have it back!"

Chapter Four
The Gnomes of Flowerdew Garden

Hob's pointed ears drooped in dismay. "That's all very well – but we can't get to Flowerdew Garden with all these sinkholes in the way."

"We can find a way if we work together," said Glitterhoof.

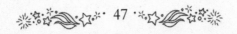

"Glitterhoof's right," said Aisha. "Hob,
you could push the cart while Glitterhoof
pulls it. Emily and I will keep back the
vines. We can do it!"

They got to work. The cart lurched
between the sinkholes, Glitterhoof gritting
her teeth with the effort as she heaved it
along. Hob pushed and caught any jars
and bottles that were jolted off, while
Emily and Aisha used large sticks to

whack the vines away. Soon everyone
was hot and sweaty, but they'd made it to
the other side.

"Bless my stars!" said Hob, mopping
his face with his hat. "I'm so glad we
bumped into each other."

There was a winding path up to the
garden door. As they walked along it,
Emily's eye was caught by a clump of
foxgloves with orange blooms. She gave
a gasp – the flowers
were shaped like tiny
fox heads! "Amazing!
I've never seen these
in any of my science
books!"

She and Aisha

leaned in for a closer look.

"Grrrrr!" The foxgloves were growling at them! The girls took a hasty step back.

"Careful, girls!" Hob said. "The plants here guard Flowerdew Garden from intruders – so don't touch anything! I'll lead the way."

They carried on, Hob in front, followed by the girls, then Glitterhoof pulling the cart. The little goblin hurried them past a plant with a candyfloss scent and green pods hanging from its stems. "It's a sweet-dream pea," he said. "Mind you don't sniff it too deeply, or you'll nod off into a magical sleep!" After the sweet-dream pea was a bush of red fruits that looked like raspberries, but were as sticky as chewing gum. "Glue gums," Hob explained. Emily used a leaf to carefully pull one out of Glitterhoof's tail.

The girls gasped as they came around the next curve in the path. In front of them was a plant as big as the cart. It looked like a huge, pink open mouth with pointed green teeth around the edges. In the centre of the mouth was something shiny.

"That looks scary," said Aisha, peering at the plant's teeth.

"Don't worry," said Emily, "it only eats flies! We've got them in our world, too – it's a Venus flytrap."

"Close, my dear," said Hob, "but this is actually a Venus spytrap. It spies thieves

who want to steal
things from the
garden. It uses sparkly
things to trap them,
you see."

They had almost
reached the door into
the walled garden. It
was painted green and
decorated with carvings of leaves. Aisha
pointed to a plant growing beside it with
tiny blue blossoms. "What does that one
do, Hob?"

He adjusted his spectacles. "Oh, this
one is perfectly safe!" Hob picked a sprig.
"It's just a very ordinary, utterly harmless,
forget-me-n …" He trailed off. Blue

smoke suddenly swirled around him.

When it cleared, Hob peered at the girls
and Glitterhoof, then he took his hat off
and gave a little bow. "Good afternoon,
dear strangers! Could you tell me where
I am?"

Aisha and Emily stared at him in
confusion.

"Oh no," said Glitterhoof. "That plant
wasn't harmless – it's made him forget
everything!"

The girls gave groans of dismay. "What
are we going to do?" wondered Aisha.

"Flowerdew Garden doesn't just
contain magical plants," said Glitterhoof
thoughtfully. "It's also where the gnomes
live. They have their own magic, and they

know about all the different plants in Enchanted Valley. Perhaps they can help Hob get his memory back …"

She knocked on the garden door with the tip of her horn.

For a moment, nothing happened. Then a slot near the bottom of the door opened to reveal the face of a very little person.

Her skin was the colour of rich earth, her eyes were blue and she had pointed ears. On her head was a bluebell hat.

The girls exchanged excited grins. They had never met a gnome before!

Glitterhoof bent down to speak to her. "Hello, Bluebell. These are my friends Aisha and Emily. Please could we come into your garden? We need your help."

Bluebell beamed. "Of course you can!" she said.

Immediately, the door to the garden swung open. Glitterhoof pulled the cart, while Emily and Aisha took Hob's hands, and they all went inside.

The girls gasped. The garden was beautiful, full of flowerbeds spilling over with blooms. Flowers in every colour grew up the walls, over wooden archways and across the backs of little benches dotted around the carpet of soft lawn. The air was sweet with delicate scents, and butterflies darted among the blooms. Tending the flowers were busy gnomes, each wearing a flower-shaped hat and pushing their own little wheelbarrow.

"Welcome to Flowerdew Garden," said Bluebell in a tinkling voice. Now they could see that she was wearing overalls in the same blue as her hat, and blue wellies. Like all the other gnomes, she was tiny – even smaller than Hob.

"This is Primrose, our head gardener," Bluebell said, as a gnome wearing a

yellow flower hat with matching overalls and wellies came over, pushing her wheelbarrow.

"Hello there," said Primrose. "How can we help?"

Quickly, the girls and Glitterhoof explained what had happened – from Selena stealing Glitterhoof's locket, right up to Hob losing his memory.

Primrose frowned, her face wrinkling like a little brown berry. "We heard that Selena had been up to no good again," she said. "Of course we'll help get the locket back. But first, let's fix poor Hob. He's always forgetting not to sniff the forget-mes …" She began rummaging inside her wheelbarrow.

Emily gazed around at the garden. "That's funny … The other plants in Enchanted Valley are suffering, but all the ones here seem fine!"

"It's the walls surrounding the garden," said Bluebell. "They're magical and keep everything inside them safe."

"That's good," said Aisha, then she gave a sigh. "But all the sinkholes outside made us think the locket must be here. I guess we were wrong."

Primrose was still searching through her wheelbarrow. She picked up a paper packet. "No, those are Speedy Seeds … Hmm, the Shrinking Can makes things smaller, and the Blooming Can makes them bigger, so those won't help …" She moved two watering cans aside, then picked up a spade. "The Flower Finder won't help either … Aha!" She pulled out a pot with a blue flower growing inside.

Primrose showed the flower to Hob, who took a sniff. Blue sparkles began to swirl around him. Emily and Aisha held their breath, hoping it would work …

As the sparkles faded, Hob took off his spectacles and rubbed his eyes. "Dancing dandelions," he murmured. "Hello there, Primrose! And hello, girls and Glitterhoof!"

"Hooray!" cheered Aisha.

"You remember us!" Emily added, as the girls hugged him.

"Of course I do," said Hob, putting his spectacles back on. "But what happened?"

"You picked a forget-me by mistake," said Emily. "We're still looking for Glitterhoof's locket, Hob. We don't know where ..." She trailed off as  she noticed something strange. One of the butterflies fluttering on a rose bush was much larger than the others. Its antennae were made from two sticks. Orange paint was peeling from its wings, revealing black underneath ...

"Aaaaah-choooo!" sneezed the butterfly.

"That's not a butterfly at all," said Primrose.
"In fact, it looks more like a bat …"

"Watch out," cried Emily. "It's Flit!"

Chapter Five
The Shrinking Can

"Aaaaah-choooo!" Flit sneezed again, and the twigs flew off his head. Around his neck he still wore Glitterhoof's locket. "Sebena will be pleased wib me! Now I can get bid of all the horrible magical plants in this garden!"

"I don't know how he got into the

garden!" cried Bluebell. "The magic walls should have stopped him!"

Flit zoomed in a circle, squeaking in delight. "Nobody saw me sneak in when der door opened! Cleber me! Aaaaah-aaaah-CHOOOO!"

The enormous sneeze sent him sprawling into a patch of daisies – and the locket flew from his neck!

Aisha sprang after it, her hands cupped together like she was catching a cricket ball. But the locket sailed through her fingers and landed on a square of grass. The garden trembled, making everyone stumble – then the ground crumbled. The soil fell away to create a sinkhole, and the locket tumbled inside!

All the gnomes stared at the hole, eyes wide with horror. "Our beautiful garden!" wailed a gnome in a daffodil hat.

The girls and Glitterhoof peered over the edge of the dark sinkhole. It was about as deep as the girls were tall. The locket glinted at the bottom.

"Don't worry, everyone!" said Aisha. "I can jump down and get it."

"You'll have to be quick, Aisha!"

said Glitterhoof, pointing her horn to where vines like octopus tentacles were springing up around the sinkhole.

Aisha crouched, ready to spring.

"Look, I bound der gnomes' Shrinking Can!" said Flit, from above. They looked up. In his claws was a watering can. "Bis will stop boo!"

"Run!" shouted Primrose.

The girls and Glitterhoof began to scramble away, but it was too late – Flit tipped the Shrinking Can over them.

"Urgh!" cried Emily, as the girls' hair and clothes were soaked through. The magical water made their skin feel tingly, and they stared down at themselves as they shrank smaller and smaller. They

were soon the
same height as
the gnomes, and
Glitterhoof was the size of a
cat. The flowers around them
seemed huge now – and the
sinkhole was enormous.

"There's no way
I can jump down
now," said Aisha
with a groan. "It's
deeper than a diving
pool!"

Glitterhoof's violet
eyes were wide.
"What are we going
to do?"

Primrose ran over. "Don't worry!" she said. "We can fix this! Hob," she called, "we need my Blooming Can! It'll make them grow again!"

Hob dashed to where Primrose had left her wheelbarrow. But Flit was faster – he snatched up the Blooming Can and sprinkled it over the vines growing around the sinkhole, sniffing and giggling gleefully.

The vines shot up. Within seconds, each was as thick as a tree trunk, circling the sinkhole in a twisting, writhing forest. On one side of the vines stood the girls, Glitterhoof and Primrose – and on the other side was everyone else.

"We're trapped!" cried Primrose.

Emily turned back to the yawning darkness of the sinkhole. She took a deep breath. "There's only one way to put everything right," she said. "We've got to climb down there and get the locket."

Aisha and Primrose nodded. Glitterhoof began to tremble. "I r-r-really want to help," she said, her violet eyes filling with tears. "B-b-but it's so dark!" Aisha put her arms around Glitterhoof's neck, while Emily stroked her silky lilac mane.

"We'll need a lookout in case Flit does anything else," said Aisha. "Could you do that instead?"

Glitterhoof nodded gratefully.

"I'll go first and find the safest way down," said Aisha. "It'll be just like the

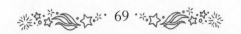

climbing wall at the gym!"

"Be careful!" said Emily.

Aisha lowered herself over the edge of the sinkhole, feeling around with her trainers for nooks to place her feet. Emily went next, then Primrose, while Glitterhoof stood guard at the edge.

Down they climbed into the darkness...

Chapter Six
Frightening Flowers

"Glitterhoof was right," said Emily with a shiver. "It is a bit scary in here."

The girls and Primrose were climbing down the sinkhole. Now that Emily and Aisha were gnome-sized, the roots and stones they used as handholds and footholds seemed huge. The further

down they
climbed, the
darker it
became,
until they could hardly see
at all.

Aisha called up instructions
as they went. "Watch out for this
bit!" she said, scrambling around a
thorny root that snagged on her shirt.
"And there's a sharp stone coming up on
your left!"

She stretched her right foot down,
searching the wall of the sinkhole for a
foothold. But here the earth was smooth.
She switched feet – but still had no luck.
"Weird," she muttered. She could feel that

below them, the wall had begun to slope like a giant slide. "We'll have to slide the rest of the way!" she called.

Aisha let go, whizzing down and giggling as she landed on a clump of round, white, springy cushions. Next came Emily, skidding to a stop beside Aisha. Then Primrose landed next to them.

Aisha bounced up and down on the strange cushions. "These feel like marshmallows! All that climbing has made me hungry …" She broke a piece off.

"No, stop!" cried Primrose. "They're not marshmallows – they're mushrooms! Look here." She tapped the edge of one of them. Emily and Aisha peered through the gloom and saw clusters of pale grey spots. "This kind are called tummy troublers," Primrose explained. "If you eat them you'll be ill."

Aisha dropped the piece of mushroom.

Emily shuddered. "I don't like it down here," she said, glancing around at the shadowy darkness. "Let's hurry up and find the locket so we can leave."

The girls and Primrose searched the bottom of the sinkhole. It was covered with pebbles that seemed as large as melons, and they had to be careful not to trip. As their eyes adjusted to the darkness, Emily and Aisha noticed lots of other plants beside the mushrooms.

"There are some more forget-mes," said Emily, showing the others a patch of the tiny blue blooms. Beside them grew tall yellow flowers with scaly petals that snapped open and closed.

"Snapdragons," said Primrose. "Watch out – they've got a nasty bite."

"Where have all these horrible plants come from?" wondered Aisha. "When we first looked into the sinkhole, there wasn't anything inside it except the locket."

"Selena's wicked magic must have done

this," said Emily. "It's making all the dangerous plants grow, and really fast!"

They carefully searched through a clump of growling foxgloves and then a bush of glue gums.

"Look!" Aisha cried. "There's something there!"

Stuck in the centre of the glue gum bush was something shiny.

"It must be the locket!" cried Emily. "We just need to get it out!"

Excitement raced through both the girls. Primrose took off her yellow flower hat and carefully leaned into the bush. Using her hat as a scoop, she pulled the glinting object out.

Emily and Aisha's excitement deflated

like burst balloons. It wasn't the locket.

Aisha groaned. "It's just a little spade," she said.

But Primrose grinned at them. "It's no ordinary little spade," she said, "it's my Flower Finder! It will take you to whatever plant you need. One of the vines must have knocked it down here." She tucked it under her arm. "It might come in handy!"

They continued the search, peering under bushes covered in thorns and through patches of nettles. Primrose went to check another big

patch of forget-mes, while the girls made
their way to the centre of the sinkhole.
There they found a huge plant like a
gaping mouth, edged with sharp green
teeth.

"A Venus spytrap!" said both girls
together.

And gleaming in the centre of the
plant's deadly pink mouth was the locket.

"Yes!" cried Aisha.
She reached towards it.
"Be careful," said
Emily, her hands
clasped to her
mouth.
"I've got to try,"
said Aisha. She leaned

in, her arm muscles stretching. Her hand was almost touching the locket. "Nearly … got it …"

Aisha leaned in a little more. Her fingers brushed the locket's chain … and the spytrap lunged forwards, snapping its enormous jaws shut. Emily gasped in shock. Aisha was trapped inside!

Chapter Seven
Tickle-Me-Pink

"Let her out!" Emily shouted. She pulled at the spytrap's jaws, but they had clamped firmly shut.

Primrose ran up and pulled at them too – but it was no good. "Aisha won't be hurt in there," she told Emily, "but I don't know how we're going to get her out.

We usually use a potion to make flowers open, but I haven't got any down here..."

"Aisha, we'll rescue you!" Emily called. "Just hang on!"

She whirled around, scanning the dark bottom of the sinkhole. There had to be something here that would help ...

On the ground lay Primrose's Flower Finder spade, where she had dropped it to try to open the jaws. Emily picked it up. "Maybe we can prise the spytrap open..."

But the spade suddenly glowed golden – then yanked Emily away from the spytrap.

"Hey!" she cried in surprise. The spade glowed again, and pulled her further

away. She clung on to the handle,
running to keep up. "Stop!" she cried. "I
need to open the spytrap!"

Primrose ran after Emily, holding on to
her yellow hat. "It's helping, Emily!" she
called. "Let it lead you – it's taking us to
the plant we need!"

The spade led them through the
darkness to a shaggy pink bush, with long,
feathery leaves. With a clang, the spade
dropped down in front of it.

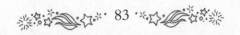

Emily panted for breath. "This must be the one that will help us free Aisha!"

Primrose caught her arm. "Be careful," she warned. "It's a tickle-me-pink – it wraps people up in its leaves and tickles them silly!"

Moving very slowly and carefully, so the branches wouldn't brush her arm, Emily reached into the bush and plucked one of the feathery leaves. As she pulled it out, another leaf brushed her wrist, fluttering around it like tickling fingers.

"Hee!" Emily giggled. "It really does tickle!"

The tickle-me-pink leaves began waving about, like long arms trying to grab them. Emily and Primrose dodged them and hurried back to the spytrap.

Holding out the leaf, Emily brushed it against the closed green teeth. "Please work," she whispered.

But the spytrap stayed firmly closed. Emily bit her lip with disappointment.

"Try tickling it underneath," said Primrose. "I'm most ticklish on my tummy – maybe the spytrap is too!"

"Good idea!" said Emily. "Here goes ..." She stroked

the leaf against the bottom of the plant —
and it began to jiggle! It shook from side
to side, exactly like someone trying not
to laugh. Emily kept tickling. Then, with
a big *POP*, the spytrap's jaws burst open.
Out on to the ground tumbled Aisha.

"Hooray!" cheered Emily and Primrose.

Aisha got to her feet. "Phew, thanks! It
was pretty hot in there. But look!" She
held out her hand.

In her palm was Glitterhoof's locket! They all gazed at it in wonder. Because the girls had shrunk, the locket seemed the size of an orange. They could see every detail of the flower growing inside the glass – the purple petals speckled with white and yellow dots, the delicate leaves curling from the stem, and the roots as fine as cobwebs.

"Now we just need to get it back to Glitterhoof!" said Emily.

They hurried to the foot of the sinkhole wall. Aisha scanned it for handholds, but the smooth, sloping sides were impossible to grab on to. Aisha groaned. "What are we going to do? We can't slide back up…"

Emily peered at the top of the sinkhole, hoping to find some way out. But just then, a shadow appeared over the entrance – and swooped down towards them! "Something's coming!" she cried. "Hide!"

"This way!" yelled Primrose.

Aisha and Emily sprinted after her. Primrose ducked beneath one of the tummy-troubler mushrooms and the girls scrambled under too. They held their breaths.

Thud! Thud, thud, thud!

Whatever had flown into the sinkhole had landed on the ground.

Her heart thumping, Aisha peeked out from under the mushroom. She could see four legs, and the swish of a lilac tail …

She turned to the others, grinning with relief. "It's Glitterhoof!"

Chapter Eight
Glitterhoof to the Rescue!

"Glitterhoof!" cried Emily. The girls and Primrose crawled out from under the mushrooms and ran to the unicorn. They threw their arms around her long neck. "You came!" said Emily. "But isn't it too dark down here for you?"

Glitterhoof nuzzled them with her silky

nose. "I had to see if you were all right," she explained. "I realised I was even more worried about my friends than I was about the dark!"

Primrose hugged her again. "That was very brave of you."

"It certainly was," agreed Aisha. "And Glitterhoof – look what we found!" She held up the locket.

"We'll put it on you as soon as we're out of the sinkhole," said Emily. "We don't want it to close up while we're still down here!"

"Oh, thank you so much!" said Glitterhoof. Her violet eyes shone with happiness. "Now, who would like a lift?"

Moments later, the girls and Primrose were on the unicorn's back, holding on tight as she flew up and out of the sinkhole. As soon as they burst from darkness into bright sunshine, Aisha leaned forwards and fastened the locket around Glitterhoof's neck.

At once, the unicorn's horn glowed green and purple, and a shower of shimmering sparkles fell all around them.

The garden transformed – the vines
shrank back into the ground, and the
sinkhole closed over. The crowd of
watching gnomes cheered and waved

their flower hats
in the air. Hob
linked arms
with Bluebell
and they
danced a jig.

The girls and
Primrose waved back at the gnomes as
Glitterhoof circled the garden, weaving in
and out of the flower beds. The blossoms
seemed the size of footballs to the girls,
and the butterflies fluttering around them
were as big as blackbirds!

Glitterhoof landed on the grass where the sinkhole had been, in front of Hob and the gnomes. Bluebell was holding a Blooming Can. She sprinkled it over the girls and Glitterhoof. Emily and Aisha felt their skin fizzle all over once more, and soon they were back to their normal size.

"You saved Flowerdew Garden!" cried Bluebell, hugging them.

"My dears, you saved all the plants of Enchanted Valley!" said Hob, his eyes twinkling behind his spectacles. The gnomes cheered again.

Primrose found her wheelbarrow and pulled out two packets. "Speedy Seeds," she explained, giving the packets to Aisha and Emily, "to say thank you."

"Please come back to our garden whenever you like!" added Bluebell.

The girls hugged them both. They were just about to leave, when one of the rose bushes began to shake.

"Aaaaah-choooo!" Flit shot out from the flowers. His nose was very red and his eyes were watery. He sat on the lawn, rubbing his face with his wings. "Bese horrible flowers are still here!" He sniffed. "You girls – aaaaah-choooo – ruined

 – aaaaah-choooo – ebberybing!" He flapped away over the garden wall.

"Poor Flit," said Emily, when the little bat was gone. "He's been really naughty, but I can't help feeling sorry for him."

"He looked so unhappy," agreed Aisha. "Maybe he would like the flowers if they didn't make him sneeze."

The girls grinned at each other as they both had the same idea.

"Hob," said Emily, "would you make a potion for us … ?"

Later that afternoon, the girls and Glitterhoof were back in the palace garden. The sinkhole had vanished – instead, cherry tree blossoms hung in fluffy pompoms and every leaf and flower was bright with colour. The four

Nature Unicorns, Queen Aurora and the girls were gathered on the soft lawn. In her dungarees pocket, Emily had a little bottle Hob had prepared for them with ingredients from Flowerdew Garden.

"I'm so proud of you, girls," Queen Aurora said. "Thank you for finding the third locket!"

"We couldn't have done it without Glitterhoof," said Aisha.

"She was so brave," added Emily. "We'd never have got out of the sinkhole without her."

Glitterhoof's horn glowed purple with happiness – but then she looked up at the sky in alarm. The girls turned to see thunderclouds sweeping towards the palace … followed by Selena!

The silver unicorn landed on the lawn, lightning crackling up and down her horn. She stamped her hooves and her purple eyes flashed. By her side hovered Flit.

"Go away, Selena," said Queen Aurora. "You've caused enough trouble!"

"Well, the trouble isn't over yet!" snapped Selena. "You girls may have

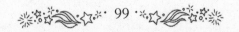

found the Earth locket, but I've still got one more … and you'll never get it back! Isn't that right, Flit?"

"Aaaaah-choooo!" went Flit. "Aaaaah-choooo! Aaaaah-choooo! Aaaaah-CHOOO!"

Aisha and Emily glanced at each other. Now was their chance!

Emily took out the bottle Hob had given them from her pocket and sprinkled the pale blue mixture inside over Flit.

The little bat shook his wings. "What's that?" he said, sniffing the droplets suspiciously. "What have you put on me?"

The girls grinned at him. "Notice anything?" asked Aisha.

Flit's eyes widened. "I'm not sneezing!

You've cured me!" He flapped his wings in excitement and sniffed at a rose bush. "Oooh! It's actually quite nice!"

Selena stamped her hooves again. "Stop messing about with those nasty flowers, Flit! We're going!" She leaped into the air and flew over the palace wall. Flit flapped after her with a cherry blossom tucked behind one of his ears.

The thunderclouds cleared again, leaving sunny blue skies. "We'll have to get Sparklesplash's locket back soon," said

Queen Aurora, "but for now let's have some fun. Would you girls like to make flower crowns?"

"Yes, please!" said Emily and Aisha together.

They all gathered around the table. Glitterhoof used her horn to magically weave blossoms together, and explained to the girls how to make them into crowns. Aisha made a crown of pink cherry blossoms, while Emily used yellow tulips. Then the girls made crowns for each of the unicorns to wear around their horns. The garden rang with laughter.

Eventually, it was time to go. The girls hugged each of the unicorns in turn.

"Goodbye!" called Emily and Aisha.

"Goodbye!" called Glitterhoof. "And thank you!"

"I'll summon you again very soon," said Queen Aurora, "so you can help us find the remaining stolen locket." Then her horn glowed, sunshine spilling out of it and around the girls. Colourful sparkles shimmered all about them and Enchanted Valley faded away …

When the light disappeared, the girls

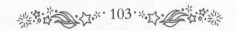

were standing in the rainy garden of Enchanted Cottage.

"What an amazing adventure," sighed Emily.

"Brilliant," agreed Aisha. She put her hand to her hair. Her flower crown had vanished, but then she remembered something else … She took her Speedy Seeds from her pocket. Emily smiled, and the two girls sprinkled their packets of seeds into one of the flowerbeds. As soon as rain fell on the seeds, flowers burst out from the soil. The girls watched in amazement as they formed a rainbow of blossoms, from red through to violet.

"What lovely flowers!" said Mrs Khan, who was coming out of the back door.

She opened an umbrella and walked across the lawn. "But I don't remember seeing them before. It's as if they've appeared by magic!"

As the two girls stood with her under the umbrella, they grinned at each other. If only she knew!

The End

Join Emily and Aisha
for another adventure in …
Sparklesplash Meets
the Mermaids
Read on for a sneak peek!

"Look, Mum!" exclaimed Aisha Khan.
"There they are!"

She pointed to three figures appearing
at the far end of the sunny little meadow.
Aisha took off, feeling the summer
dandelions tickling her shins. In a flash,
she was standing by the side of Emily
Turner, her best friend.

"My goodness," said Mrs Turner, who
stood next to Mr Turner, holding a picnic
basket on one arm. "You're a very fast
runner, Aisha!"

Emily laughed. "Aisha's good at all

sports, Mum!"

"Almost as good as Emily is at science,"
Aisha replied, smiling. "Come on. My
parents are setting up by the river. And
I have a special surprise!"

Emily and Aisha skipped through the
grass to where Mr and Mrs Khan waited
by a checked blanket laid out in a pool
of sunshine next to a sparkling river. Then
they watched nervously as the Khans
shook hands with the Turners. They
hoped their parents would get along as
well as they did!

"Pleasure to meet you both," said Mrs
Khan. "We love having Emily over at
Enchanted Cottage."

"We've heard wonderful things from

Emily," Mr Turner replied. "It sounds like an amazing place."

Emily and Aisha glanced at each other. Enchanted Cottage was where the Khans had moved when they arrived in Spellford Village only a few weeks ago. And it was an amazing place, from the phoenix statue that stood in the garden to the unicorn door-knocker. It was also a house with a wonderful secret …

"Look what I've brought!" Aisha said, picking up a piece of tupperware. She opened it to reveal a baker's dozen of brightly iced biscuits shaped like unicorns.

Emily gasped. "They're great, Aisha!"

"They match your keyring," said Mrs Turner. "You girls love your unicorns, don't you?"

Emily and Aisha giggled. If only Mrs Turner knew that the first time Emily had visited Enchanted Cottage, she and Aisha had found a crystal unicorn in the attic.

When sunlight had struck the little statue, they'd been whisked off to Enchanted Valley, a wonderful land of dragons, phoenixes and other fantastic creatures.

Read
Sparklesplash Meets the Mermaids
to find out what adventures are in store for Aisha and Emily!

Also available

Book One:

Book Two:

Book Three:

Book Four:

Unicorn Magic

Look out for the next book!

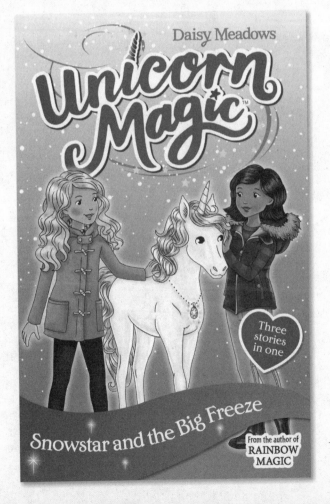

Daisy Meadows

Unicorn Magic™

Three stories in one

Snowstar and the Big Freeze

From the author of RAINBOW MAGIC

If you like
Unicorn Magic,
you'll love...

Welcome to Animal Ark!

Animal-mad Amelia is sad
about moving house, until she
discovers Animal Ark, where vets look
after all kinds of animals in need.

Join Amelia and her friend Sam for a
brand-new series of animal adventures!